Nice Try,
Tooth Fairy

Nice Try, Tooth Fairy

By Mary W. Olson

Illustrated by Katherine Tillotson

Simon & Schuster Books for Young Readers

BWI   15.00   6/03

SIMON & SCHUSTER BOOKS FOR YOUNG READERS
An imprint of Simon & Schuster Children's Publishing Division
1230 Avenue of the Americas, New York, New York 10020
Text copyright © 2000 by Mary W. Olson
Illustrations copyright © 2000 by Katherine Tillotson
All rights reserved including the right of reproduction in whole or in part in any form.
SIMON & SCHUSTER BOOKS FOR YOUNG READERS is a trademark of Simon & Schuster.
Book design by Lily Malcom
The text for this book is set in Lemonade.
The illustrations are rendered in oil.
Printed in Hong Kong
4 6 8 10 9 7 5 3
Library of Congress Cataloging-in-Publication Data
Olson, Mary W.
Nice try, Tooth Fairy / by Mary W. Olson ; illustrated by Katherine Tillotson.
p.   cm.
Summary: Hoping to get back her lost tooth, Emma writes a series of letters to the Tooth Fairy,
but when the wrong teeth keep getting returned the mistakes create complications.
ISBN 0-689-82422-X
[1. Teeth—Fiction. 2. Tooth Fairy—Fiction. 3. Letters—Fiction.] I. Tillotson, Katherine, ill. II. Title.
PZ7.O5213Ni 2000
[Fic]—dc21
98-22749
CIP   AC

To my husband, Doug, and my
two boys, Eric and Michael,
for all their love and support
—M. W. O.

To my parents,
Henry and Elizabeth
—K. T.

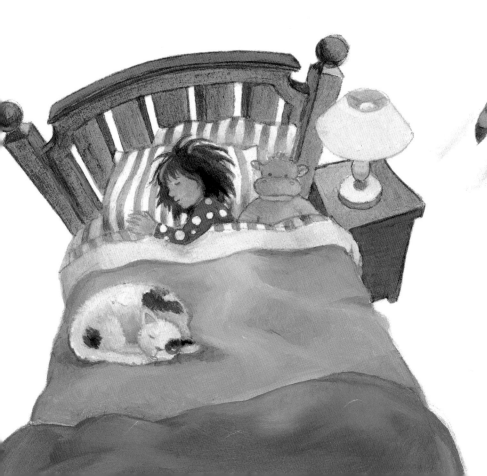

Dear Tooth Fairy,
  My grandfather is here for a visit. Could you please return my tooth so I could show it to him? Just for one day?

                              Emma

Dear Tooth Fairy,
You don't have to worry about taking back that tooth. Last night I had a surprise visitor. That tooth fit him just fine. Have you found my tooth yet?

Emma

Dear Tooth Fairy,
    No, my tooth isn't this small, either. I almost didn't see it under my pillow. Just as I was about to pick it up, a funny-looking creature tumbled through my window and grabbed it. I guess it was his.

                    Emma

Dear Tooth Fairy,
    No, that tusk's not mine,
either. Not unless you think
I'm an elephant! And
speaking of elephants,
there's one trumpeting on
my front lawn now. Do you
think this might be his?

Emma

Dear Tooth Fairy,

You sure must have a lot of teeth there. My mother says the tooth you left me last night is an alligator tooth. I'm looking for a place to put it so he'll be sure to find it!

Here's a picture of my tooth, in case you forgot what it looked like.

Emma

DEAR
TOOTH FAIRY.
HERE IS MY
FIRST TOOTH.
YOUR
FRIEND
HENRY

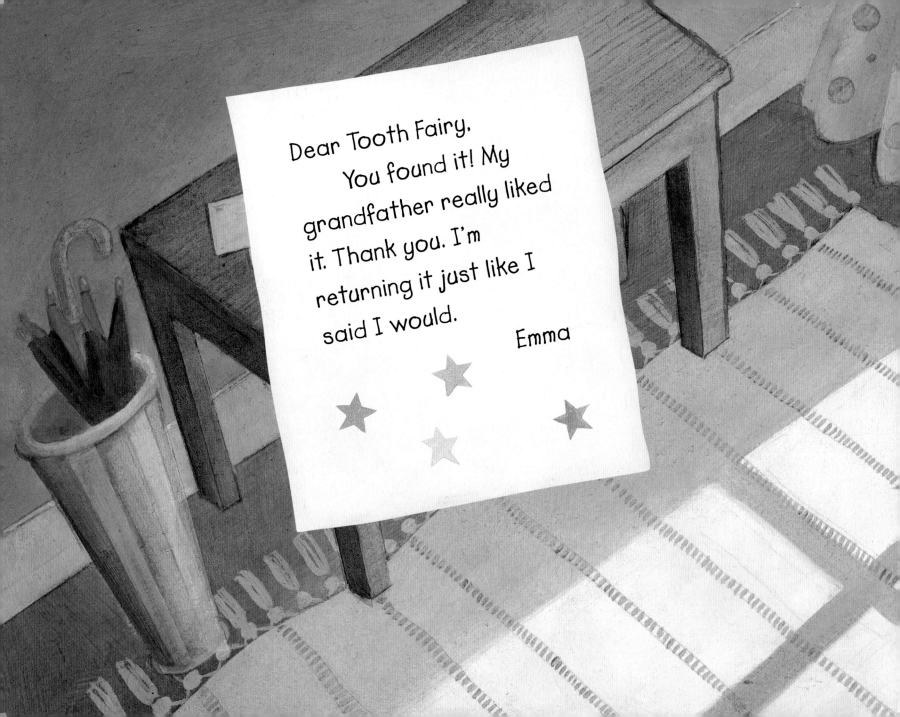

C.1